THE CLASSIC
FAIRY TALE COLLECTION

Rumpelstiltskin

Retold by John Cech
Illustrated by Martin Hargreaves

STERLING
New York / London

ONCE THERE LIVED a poor miller who had a very beautiful daughter.

One day the king was passing the mill and decided
to stop for a rest. The miller served him some
cheese and bread that he had made from
the grain he ground at his mill.
The king thought the miller's
bread was delicious
and told him so.

"Thank you, Your Majesty," replied the miller, puffing out his chest with pride. "I also have a beautiful daughter who can spin straw into gold!"

Now the mention of gold really got the king's attention. You see, although the king already had plenty of money, he still wanted more. And so he asked the miller to bring his daughter to the palace the following day.

"Your father says that you can spin gold from straw," the king said when the young woman arrived.

"That's only my father's way of saying how proud he is of me," the miller's daughter replied. "I'm afraid that he may have been stretching the truth a bit."

But the king waved her explanation aside. Instead, he showed her to a little room high up in one of the castle towers. The whole room was filled with straw, except for one corner where there stood a spinning wheel and a stool.

"I'm sure you will make good on your father's boast," said the king. "I will be back in the morning. If you can spin this straw into gold, all will be well for you and your family. If you can't, who knows what may happen." With his words still hanging in the air, the king shut and locked the door on the miller's daughter and the room full of straw.

The young woman sat in the tower room for quite some time and then she began to cry. She wanted to help her family, but she could not possibly do what the king commanded.

$\mathcal{S}$uddenly she felt a slight movement in the room. She turned to the door, and there stood a little man. Despite the door's squeaky hinges, he had entered the room without making a sound. The man had a bushy beard, bulging eyes, and hair that stood straight up on his head. He was a very strange fellow indeed. He asked the miller's daughter why she was crying, and she told him.

"Ah, that's not a problem," said the little man. "What will you give me if I spin this straw into gold for you?"

"I have a necklace made of stones polished by the sea. It was a gift from my father, but I would gladly give it to you."

"Done!" he said, and set himself to work on the small stool in the corner.

The little man spun all night, and by morning a pile of golden threads
had replaced the straw. The miller's daughter was still dozing when the
king opened the door and found, to his amazement, that the young woman
had done what her father had boasted. But instead of sending her home
with a splendid reward, the king showed the young woman to
another, larger room, filled with even more straw.

"Since you have done so well once, I know you will be able to do it again."
The miller's daughter told the king that she could not do as he commanded,
but he reminded her to think of the fate that might await her and her family
if she failed. Then he left the room, locking the door behind him.

The miller's daughter threw herself onto the straw and wept herself to sleep. When she awoke, the little man had appeared once more.

"Pish-posh," he said when she told him of her latest task. "There's nothing to cry about. I can spin this straw into gold by morning, but what will you give me in return for my labors?"

"I have a ring," the miller's daughter replied. "My mother gave it to me before she died. Here, it is yours. Please help me."

The little man happily took the ring and then spun and hummed, hummed and spun, deep into the night. Eventually, the miller's daughter dozed off. By morning, all the straw had been turned into a large, gleaming pile of golden thread, and the little man had disappeared. The king was even more astonished than before.

At last, thought the miller's daughter, *I can finally go home!* But instead, the king led her to an even larger room, this time filled to the ceiling with straw. "If you can change all of this into gold, you can return to your family. But if you can't . . . well, things will not go so well," he said ominously as he left the room and turned the key in the lock.

Alone in the room, the miller's daughter fell into despair. This task was even more impossible than the others had been. She was afraid of what might happen to her, but even more, she could not bear to think of what might befall her family.

But just as the castle clock struck midnight, the little man appeared in her room once again. He looked around and said, "Hmmmm. Now this will stretch my fingers. What shall be my reward?"

"I have nothing left to give you," the miller's daughter replied sadly.

"I will spin the straw into gold," said the little man, "but one day I will ask you for something in return, and you will not be able to refuse. Do you promise?"

"Oh, yes, I promise," said the miller's daughter. She thought that when the time came, she would certainly be able to think of a way to make good on her promise.

"Very well," the little man replied. "But remember, you must keep your promise."

The miller's daughter nodded in agreement and the little man set to work, spinning and humming, humming and spinning, until the miller's daughter fell asleep and the first light of day crept through the high window of the room.

The little man vanished with the sound of the first birds, leaving behind an enormous room full of gold. When the king found the glittering treasure, he was amazed. And, of course, he was in love. He had been from the moment he saw the miller's beautiful daughter. The king begged the miller's daughter to marry him, and she agreed. But she made him promise never, ever to make her spin again.

The two were soon married. More than a year passed, and they had a baby boy whom they adored. One day while the queen was in the garden with the baby, the little man stepped out from behind a rose bush.

"Remember me?" he asked. "And your promise? I have come to collect."

"What is it you want?" the queen asked.

"I have always wanted to have a child of my own," the little man said. "And since no one will marry me, I ask only for your firstborn son. You cannot break your promise, you know."

"I would rather die," replied the queen, "than give my child to you."

"I hope it won't come to that," he said. "I'll tell you what. I will give you three days. If in that time you can guess my name, we'll forget about your promise."

And in a cloud of morning mist, the little man was gone.

The queen quickly called for the royal librarian, the royal historian, and the royal messenger. She asked the first two to bring her every name they could find in the books of the royal library and every name that had ever been recorded in the kingdom. She asked the messenger to send word to the surrounding towns and villages that they should bring her the names of all the little men they knew.

At sunset, the librarian handed the queen a long list of all the names he could find. The queen stayed up late into the night studying the list. The next day, she again found the little man standing in the garden.

"So," he said. "Have you found out my name?"

"Well, let me see. Is it Allen? Henry? Mortimer? Salvatore? Claude? Ziggy?"

"No, no, no," replied the little man to each name. The queen recited hundreds and hundreds of names until finally she got to the end of the list. But the little man said no to each of them.

"I'll be back tomorrow," he said. "Maybe then you will have some better guesses."

That evening the court historian brought the queen a record of every name that had ever been officially recorded in the kingdom. She studied them all night long. The next day, when the little man appeared, the queen asked, "Are you Reginald? Sydney? Isaac? Basil? Egbert? Osgood? Cedric?"

"Indeed, I am not," he said, and shook his head with each name. When the queen had spoken the final name—which was Zachary—the little man said, "I will be back tomorrow. It will be your last chance to guess my name."

The queen was unable to sleep that night. At first light, her messenger appeared. His face was haggard and worn. He had been searching the kingdom for names all night. He told the queen all the names he had heard, but they were the same as the ones she had already repeated to the little man.

"There was one other name," the messenger said.

"But it is very unusual. I was returning to the palace through

a lonely valley in a deep forest. It was still dark when through the

trees I saw a fire. I moved in close enough to see a little man dancing

around the flames, singing an odd song."

No one knows where I was born

No one knows where I have been

No one knows where I will go

No one in the whole wide world

No one but me—Rumpelstiltskin.

"Did he have a bushy beard, bulging eyes, and shaggy black hair that stood straight up?"

"He did, Your Majesty!" replied the messenger.

The queen thanked him and sent him off for food and rest.

For the first time in days, the queen felt a ray of hope break through the clouds. She didn't have time to bask in its light, though, because the little man had suddenly appeared in the garden.

"Well," he said as he cleared his throat and rubbed his hands together. "I've come for the gift that you promised to me."

"Yes, of course," said the queen. "But I have thought of a few more names. Maybe one of them belongs to you."

"Guessing will do you no good," the little man replied. "My name is a secret from all the world."

"Then you won't mind my guessing," said the queen. "Is it Herman? Titus? Constantine? Florian?"

"Your Majesty," the little man scoffed. "I know you're trying very hard, but you aren't even close."

"How about Rumpelstiltskin?" she asked innocently.

"Wha ... wha ... wha ...," the little man sputtered. "How could you know that?! You tricked me! You tricked me!" He began to hop around on one foot and then the other. The more he hopped, the angrier he became until, fuming, he finally stomped his way right out of the garden and was never seen again.

The queen and her family lived for a long, long time. They used the gold the little man had spun to help the children, the elderly, the sick, and the homeless of the land. And whenever parents couldn't decide what to name their baby, the queen was always ready to help. After all, she knew all the names in the country and could always pick just the name that would fit a child perfectly.

About the Story

The earliest printed version of "Rumpelstiltskin" can be found in a collection of stories called "amusements" from the 1500s by the French writer François Rabelais. The source of the little man's peculiar name may have come from an old German children's game—*Rumpele stilt oder der Poppart*—which may have been played on stilts. Old engravings show children playing together, running races, and generally having a rumpus while balancing precariously on sticks of wood.

The story of "Rumpelstiltskin" that has come down to us was made famous by the Brothers Grimm, who cobbled the tale together from four previously existing versions of the story that they collected in Germany. Folktales from other countries also tell about young women in need of help with their spinning, the ancient skill that all girls were required to learn but that not all were equally good at. In the Grimms' day, it was said that the woman who could spin exceptionally well was worth her weight in gold.

Other versions of the "Rumpelstiltskin" story can be found throughout Europe, from England and Sweden to Italy and Ukraine. The little man in these tales may be a gnome, a dwarf, or another member of that family of little people who inhabit the realm of fairies. He goes by various names, all of them unusual, like the tongue trying to balance itself on verbal stilts: Purzinigele, Tarandando, Kruzimugeli, Titteli Ture, Gwarwyn-a-throt, Kinkach Martinko, Whuppity Stoorie, and Tom Tit Tot. Sometimes the little man wants the young woman's hand in marriage, sometimes he simply wants to be treated well and to remain at the young woman's side to spin for her.

Whatever the differences in how the tale has been told over the centuries, one of the common threads that weaves through all of these versions of the story is the idea of discovering the secret name of the little man. "What's in a name?" Shakespeare has Juliet ask in *Romeo and Juliet*. A great deal. Long ago, names were regarded as having magical or even sacred significance. In some religions, it is forbidden to utter the name of the Deity. Knowing someone's real name could mean—as it does in this story—that you were in possession of secret information about that person and thus had power over him. In some Native American cultures, a boy is renamed at different points in his life, depending on particular accomplishments and acts of bravery or other distinctions. Nicknames, of course, serve a similar, if not always lofty, function for our family and friends. Some of these names may even be as mysterious and unusual as any secret name from a fairy tale.

—J. C.

STERLING and the distinctive Sterling logo are registered trademarks of Sterling Publishing Co., Inc.

Library of Congress Cataloging-in-Publication Data
Cech, John.
Rumpelstiltskin / retold by John Cech ; illustrated by Martin Hargreaves.
p. cm.
Summary: A strange little man helps the miller's daughter spin straw into gold
for the king on the condition that she will give him her first-born child.
Includes historical notes on the story's origins, versions from
other countries, and the significance of names.
ISBN 978-1-4027-3066-5
[1. Fairy tales. 2. Folklore--Germany.] I. Hargreaves, Martin, ill. II.
Rumpelstiltskin (Folk tale). English. III. Title.

PZ8.C293Ru 2008
398.2--dc22
[E]
2007001780

2 4 6 8 10 9 7 5 3 1

Published by Sterling Publishing Co., Inc.
387 Park Avenue South, New York, NY 10016
Text © 2008 by John Cech
Illustrations © 2008 by Martin Hargreaves
Distributed in Canada by Sterling Publishing
c/o Canadian Manda Group, 165 Dufferin Street
Toronto, Ontario, Canada M6K 3H6
Distributed in the United Kingdom by GMC Distribution Services
Castle Place, 166 High Street, Lewes, East Sussex, England BN7 1XU
Distributed in Australia by Capricorn Link (Australia) Pty. Ltd.
P.O. Box 704, Windsor, NSW 2756, Australia

Printed in China

Sterling   ISBN 978-1-4027-3066-5

For information about custom editions, special sales, premium andcorporate purchases,
please contact Sterling Special SalesDepartment at 800-805-5489 or specialsales@sterlingpublishing.com.